P9-ARQ-201

DISCARDED

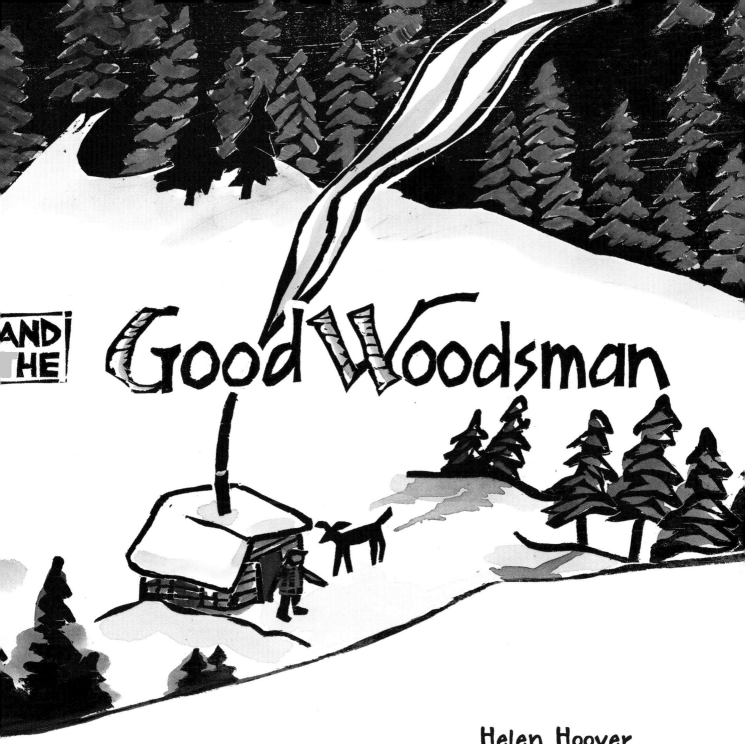

AND THE Good Woodsman

Helen Hoover

Woodcuts by Betsy Bowen

University of Minnesota Press
Minneapolis ■ London

The Fesler-Lampert Minnesota Heritage Book Series

This series reprints significant books that enhance our understanding and appreciation of Minnesota and the Upper Midwest. It is supported by the generous assistance of the John K. and Elsie Lampert Fesler Fund and the interest and contribution of Elizabeth P. Fesler and the late David R. Fesler.

Text copyright 1967 by Helen Hoover

Illustrations copyright 2005 by Betsy Bowen

Published by arrangement with The Ohio University Foundation

First University of Minnesota Press edition, 2005

All rights reserved. No part of this publication may be reproduced, stored in a retrieval system, or transmitted, in any form or by any means, electronic, mechanical, photocopying, recording, or otherwise, without the prior written permission of the publisher.

Published by the University of Minnesota Press
111 Third Avenue South, Suite 290
Minneapolis, MN 55401-2520
http://www.upress.umn.edu

Library of Congress Cataloging-in-Publication Data

Hoover, Helen.
  Great Wolf and the Good Woodsman / Helen Hoover ; woodcuts by Betsy Bowen.-- 1st University of Minnesota Press ed.
      p. cm. -- (The Fesler-Lampert Minnesota heritage book series)
  Summary: The miracle of Christmas permits the animals to work together as friends, despite their fear of the Great Wolf, and to rescue their beloved woodsman.
   ISBN 0-8166-4445-4 (hc/j : alk. paper)
  1. Wolves--Juvenile fiction. [1. Wolves--Fiction. 2. Christmas--Fiction. 3. Animals--Fiction.] I. Bowen, Betsy, ill.
II. Title. III. Series.
   PZ10.3.H7803Gr 2005
   [Fic]--dc22
                      2005000676

Printed in the United States of America on acid-free paper

The University of Minnesota is an equal-opportunity educator and employer.

12 11 10 09 08 07 06 05   10 9 8 7 6 5 4 3 2 1

To my husband, Adrian

– H. H.

To my mom, Betty Lovejoy Olsen

– B. B.

Also by Helen Hoover

Animals at My Doorstep
Animals Near and Far
The Gift of the Deer
The Long-Shadowed Forest
A Place in the Woods
The Years of the Forest

Also by Betsy Bowen

Antler, Bear, Canoe: A Northwoods Alphabet Year
Gathering: A Northwoods Counting Book
Tracks in the Wild

Illustrated by Betsy Bowen

Borealis by Jeff Humphries
Shingebiss: An Ojibwe Legend by Nancy Van Laan
The Troll with No Heart in His Body by Lise Lunge-Larsen
A Wild Neighborhood by John Henricksson

Artist's Note

My mother introduced me to Helen and Adrian Hoover in 1963 in Leng's Fountain in Grand Marais, Minnesota. My family had just started to visit the North Shore of Lake Superior from Chicago. The Hoovers' books *The Gift of the Deer* and *The Long-Shadowed Forest* colored our sense of wonder and discovery of the northwoods. The Hoovers' life on Gunflint Lake seemed mysteriously captivating.

Great Wolf and the Good Woodsman was first published in 1967. By then I was living full time on the North Shore, and my boys and I must have worn out the local library copy of the book with our many readings. I am honored to illustrate this new edition of the story I have enjoyed for so long.

Betsy Bowen

"My wild neighbors became my animal friends,
and I learned something very wonderful —
everything that grows and lives is important
to all the other things."

— Helen Hoover, *Animals at My Doorstep*

Great Wolf AND THE Good Woodsman

nce, long years ago, Great Wolf stood on a high ridge and looked down at a deer, a squirrel, and a chickadee, gathered together beside the log cabin where lived the Good Woodsman.

It was Christmas, and Great Wolf was very lonely. He was a mighty hunter, fleet of foot and sharp of tooth, and so he was feared by all the animals in the forest.

"Why doesn't the Good Woodsman come out?" the gentle deer was asking. "He always has fresh cedar branches for me to eat."

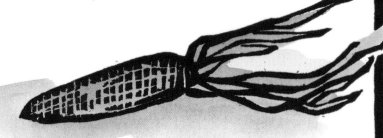

"And corn for me," chattered the squirrel.

"And seeds for me," the chickadee chirped, darting into the air. "I think something is wrong."

The squirrel scampered up the logs
to peer in the window, and gave a startled
squeak. The deer flashed to his side,
and the chickadee flew up to the windowsill.
Great Wolf moved down the slope to a place
where he, too, could see inside, and he saw the
Good Woodsman, sitting on the floor holding
his ankle.

"He's hurt," said the squirrel. "He can't
walk, and he will freeze without a fire. He
has no coat like ours to keep him warm. We
must get help!"

"There is a kind man in the house beside
the lake," said the deer. "I can run there—"

"And I can fly," added the chickadee.

"And I can chatter," said the squirrel.
"But the man will not understand us. How can
we make the man come with us?"

Great Wolf straightened up and lifted his head, proud in the knowledge that on this Christmas Day he could offer a special gift to his friend, the Good Woodsman. While the other animals stood in an anxious group, he walked slowly and silently into the clearing. "I can help you," he said as softly as he could.

The squirrel jumped onto the roof, and the deer in her fear and excitement floundered in the deep snow. Bravely, the little chickadee flew around Great Wolf's head, trying to frighten him away.

"Please don't be afraid," Great Wolf said. "Don't you know that on Christmas Day all animals are friends? The Good Woodsman has been kind to me as well as to you, and now I can help him. I will run over the hills to the house of the man who lives beside the lake. The man is my enemy, but he has a dog—and the dog and I are cousins. I will tell the dog about the Good Woodsman, and he can make his master understand." And before the animals could say a word, Great Wolf leaped away, his gray fur bright as silver in the sun, and his green eyes shining.

When he came to the house beside the lake, he saw the man chopping wood. Great Wolf hesitated, for he feared the man. But there was no time for waiting. Leaping nimbly over the gleaming ice, straight past the man he ran, toward the house where lived his cousin, the dog.

"A wolf!" cried the man. He dropped his ax and ran for his rifle. But by that time Great Wolf had already told the dog about the Good Woodsman's accident and was safely out of sight in the shadows under the trees.

The dog caught his master's pants leg in his teeth and pulled toward the path. Then he ran ahead and waited. When the man hesitated, the dog ran back to him and barked eagerly. "You want me to come with you, don't you?" the man said, turning toward his house. He came back wearing a fur-lined coat and followed the dog along the path, while Great Wolf kept pace with them through the forest.

Great Wolf hurried ahead and stood
on the slope, watching and listening. The deer
and the squirrel slipped into the shadows
when they heard the man and the dog
coming near, and the chickadee flew again to
the windowsill. The dog barked at the Good
Woodsman's door until the man opened it.

"What happened?" the man asked, helping the Good Woodsman to a chair.

"I stumbled over a piece of stovewood and twisted my ankle. It is lucky that you came by, for my fire is out and I would have surely frozen."

"It wasn't just luck," the man explained. "My dog brought me here."

"Strange," said the Good Woodsman. "I haven't seen him for several days." Then he smiled. "Perhaps one of my friends told him."

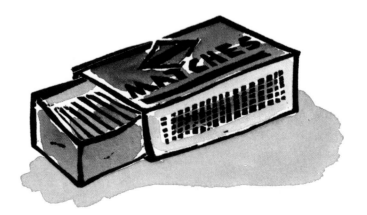

"Don't tell me your animals can talk," the man said, laughing, as he bandaged the Good Woodsman's ankle.

"Not to you, but I think your dog can understand them—at least one of them," the Good Woodsman answered. He slowly stood up and leaned on the crutch the man had made from a bent stick. "I'll be fine now, thanks."

He patted the dog. "And thank you, too!" The dog thumped his tail joyfully on the floor and barked his own special Merry Christmas to the Good Woodsman.

The Good Woodsman busied himself, hobbling about the cabin with his crutch. At last he opened the cabin door, carrying a Christmas feast of cedar and corn and seeds. The deer and the squirrel came out of the forest, and the chickadee flew down from the windowsill into a snowdrift. The Good Woodsman stood in the doorway watching his friends eat. Great Wolf, looking down from the ridge, was filled with a great gladness for them, but as he watched he grew lonelier than ever. "It is sometimes sad to be a mighty hunter, feared by all the animals," he said to himself.

Then the Good Woodsman brought out a plate of meat. "Come down, Great Wolf," he called. "Come down and have dinner with us."

Slowly Great Wolf stepped from the shadows. "Welcome, Great Wolf," whispered the deer, trembling in spite of herself.

"If it hadn't been for you," the squirrel said, "this might have been a very sad Christmas instead of a happy one."

And the chickadee perched on Great Wolf's head to sing his little song of gratitude.

"It is a very happy day for me," Great
Wolf told them, "for I have never been
invited to a Christmas dinner before."

"It is a happy day for us all," said the
Good Woodsman, smiling at his friends. "We
all have good things in us, and today Great
Wolf has had the opportunity to show us how
really great he is."

When they had finished, Great Wolf thanked the Good Woodsman, and as the others melted back into the forest he bounded away across the ridge, calling back in a long musical howl.

nd ever since that time some people say if you listen very closely to the howling of a wolf on Christmas, you will hear him call *Noooooooooo-ellllllll!* in memory of Great Wolf and the Good Woodsman. And *Noel*, after all, is really another word for Christmas.

Helen Hoover moved to the wilderness of northern Minnesota in the 1950s, interrupting forever her career as a chemical engineer in Chicago. She and her artist husband Adrian chronicled their observations and experiences at their home on Gunflint Lake in a number of well-loved books.

Betsy Bowen migrated to the northwoods as a back-to-the-lander in the 1960s and has made her home there ever since. She operates her fine-art print shop and studio in Grand Marais, Minnesota.